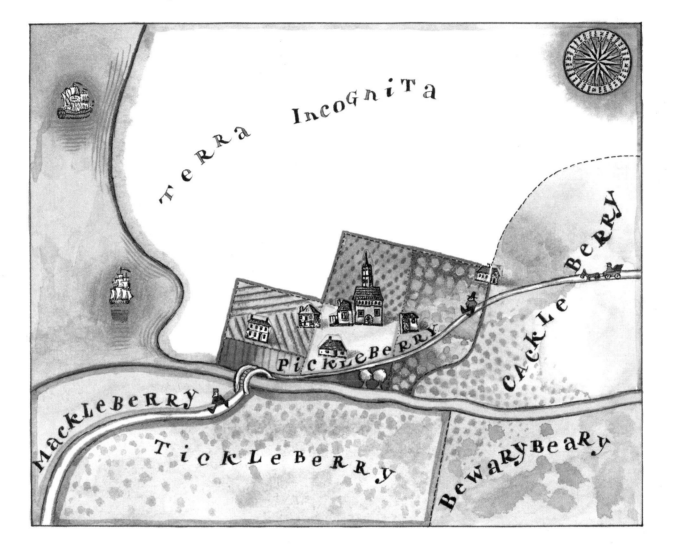

National Flag of the Empire of Pickleberry

National Sun

National Dessert—Pickle Pudding

National Moon

Nonsense is alive and well and living in Pickleberry. —Lou of Pickleberry

Uri Shulevitz

WhaT is a WiSe BiRd like you doing in a SiLLy tale like this?

FARRAR STRAUS GIROUX   NEW YORK

In memory of my mother.

I've adapted some of her stories from my childhood for this book.

10 9 8 7 6 5 4 3 2 1

Library of Congress Cataloging-in-Publication Data
Shulevitz, Uri, date.
    What is a wise bird like you doing in a silly tale like this? / Uri Shulevitz. — 1st ed.
        p.   cm.
    Summary: Relates the doings of the Emperor of Pickleberry and his ingenious talking bird Lou.
    ISBN 0-374-38300-6
    [1. Birds—Fiction. 2. Kings, queens, rulers, etc.—Fiction.] I. Title.
PZ7.S5594Wh   2000
[E]—dc21   99-31002

There once was an Emperor.

And oh what an Emperor he was! He was no ordinary Emperor, that Emperor of Pickleberry.

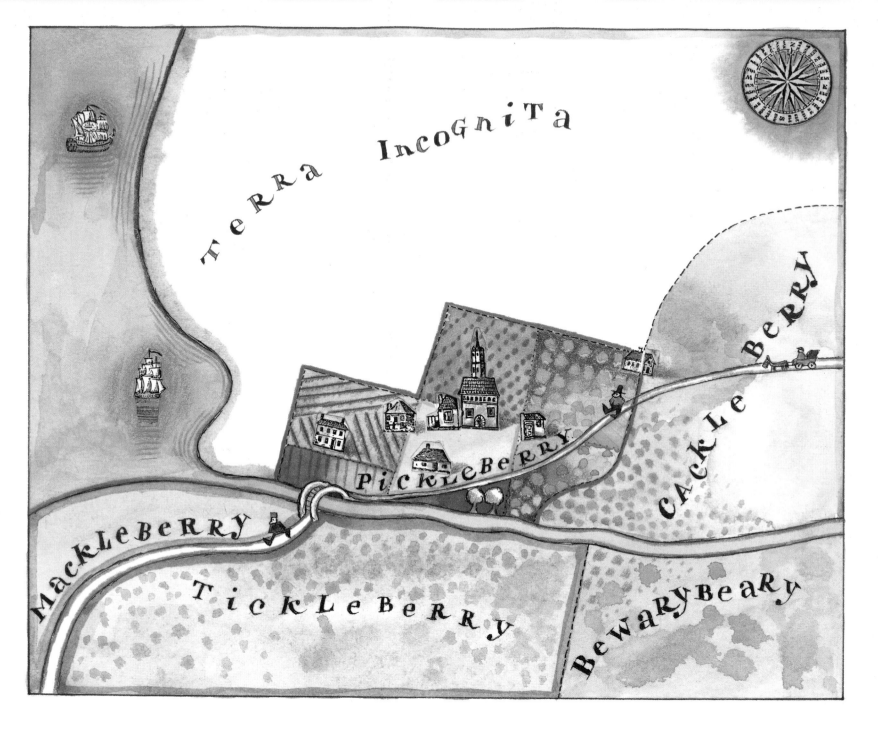

And Pickleberry was no ordinary empire either.

The Empire of Pickleberry consisted of the village of Pickleberry, four and a half acres of land,

and a population of twenty-six and a half citizens.

The half citizen was an invisible fellow with a big mustache whom everyone knew and who spoke in half words.

He lived on the border of the empire, and his house was half in Pickleberry and half in neighboring Cackleberry.

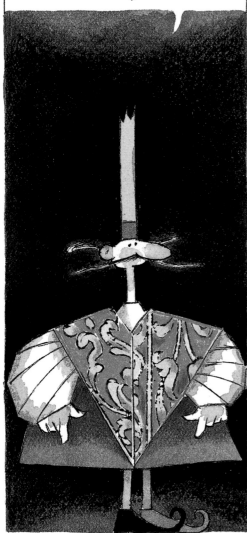

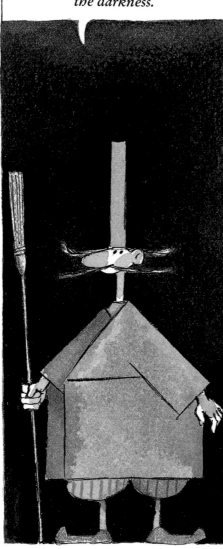

The Emperor of Pickleberry had a twin brother. It was nearly impossible to tell them apart, except that one was an Emperor and the other a janitor. But the janitor was no ordinary janitor either, since he had a broom and a brother who was Emperor.

The Emperor kept the janitor busy from dawn to dusk. He had him sweep the palace twice a day and fix broken furniture in between.

The Emperor also had a bird named Lou. And oh what a bird that Lou was! That Lou was a genius of a bird. The brightest fellow with wings who ever was. And he could talk, too.

The historians of Pickleberry couldn't agree on how Lou became such a genius. Some of them believed that the half citizen with the big mustache was a half-wit. Others were convinced that the half citizen was a genius and that Lou had studied with him.

Be that as it may, Lou was so smart that the Emperor came every day to consult him on important matters of state. Such as: "If one had an itch on a Sunday at 3:16 in the afternoon, should one scratch with the third finger of the right hand or with the second finger of the left hand?"

To which Lou answered: "It all depends on the itch." Or: "Itch me no itch, and scratch me no scratch."

To make a long story a little shorter, the Emperor treated Lou better than his own brother, the janitor. Lou was fed the most exotic, rare, and exquisite delicacies other birds may only dream about. He was given curd caramel crisp with tamatar, badam, shalgam, zafran, mari, curry, and adrak, as much as he wanted, and anything else a bird might desire. Anything, that is, except freedom. For Lou spent his days and his nights in a cage. It was no ordinary cage either, since it was a luxurious cage in the palace of Pickleberry. But it was still a cage, and Lou was not free.

One day, the Emperor was in a particularly generous mood. He bestowed a great honor on the janitor. He appointed him part-time ambassador for extraordinary missions, and ordered him to go shopping in a faraway land. Before leaving, the janitor passed by Lou's cage.

"Mr. Ambassador," said Lou. "Would you be so kind, if on your journey you should meet my Aunt Millie, to please tell her I live in a cage?"

"You can count on me, Lou," said the janitor.

While on his journey, the janitor passed through a forest. He saw Aunt Millie, and he knew at once it was Aunt Millie. And it was. Now, let it be known that Aunt Millie was even smarter than Lou.

The janitor said politely, in nearly unpronounceable and untranslatable Birdish, "Katschkadrinaminafinakuchimuchibamba, Aunt Millie." Which means, roughly, "Hi, Aunt Millie." This pleased Aunt Millie so much that, without further ado, she flew over and settled on the janitor's hat. The janitor gave her Lou's message. But no sooner had he uttered the word "cage" than Aunt Millie fainted. The janitor took her down from his hat and put her on the ground to see how he could help her. But Aunt Millie seemed beyond help. In fact, she seemed quite dead. Then, suddenly, to the janitor's amazement, Aunt Millie rose up and flew away.

When he returned to the palace, the janitor thought that Lou would be upset when he heard what had happened with Aunt Millie. But to his surprise, Lou merely thanked him, and that was that.

The next morning, when the Emperor went to hold counsel with Lou on a matter of state, he found him dead. No matter how hard he shook the cage, Lou showed no sign of life. The Emperor was furious. "How dare he die without my permission!" And he ordered the janitor to throw the bird away.

The janitor took Lou outside the palace and put him in the shade of a tree. As soon as the janitor was out of sight, Lou flew away.

Lou was happy to be free. But he was tired.

After his long stay in a cage, he wasn't accustomed to flying long distances. And so, after a short flight, he landed on a low bush to take a rest, and fell asleep.

A traveling salesman came along. He saw the sleeping bird and caught it. Counting on his fingers and toes, he said:

"One, three, ten, eleven—I'll sell him for eleven goldings! Eleven goldings makes twenty silverinos, twenty silverinos comes to ninety-six copperings, ninety-six copperings equals one hundred eighty-two bronzinos—and, presto, I buy a dozen chickens from the invisible half citizen in Cackleberry, and another dozen from him in Pickleberry. Now I have two dozen chickens. I pay two silverinos, sixty-three copperings, and four bronzinos. Each chicken lays nineteen eggs. The eggs hatch. I sell the young chickens in Mackleberry. Now, let's see: two dozen chickens times nineteen eggs comes to—three times eleven chickens—wait—or is it twelve chickens times nineteen eggs? . . . Hmm, let me count again . . . "

"Don't count your chickens before they've hatched," said Lou, and he opened his eyes.

"A talking bird—it's my lucky day!" said the salesman. "A talking bird sells for nineteen goldings—now, that's wealth!"

"Health is better than wealth," said Lou, "but sage advice is priceless. Let me go and I'll give you some advice."

"Advice is for the birds," said the salesman. "Let me give you some advice, pal: a bird in the hand is worth two in the bush." And he tightened his grip.

"Then how about some nonsense?" said Lou.

"Now you're talking," said the salesman. "Nonsense is very popular these days."

So Lou began:

"In Pickleberry, there lived twin brothers. One was an Emperor, and the other a janitor.

"One day, the Emperor decreed that raw horseradish must never be eaten with diddle-dumplings and sour spinach marmalade. Such an unjust law made the twenty-six citizens angry.

"But the invisible half citizen with the big mustache was furious. So he grabbed half a cup and threw its invisible saucer on the ground.

"This caused a tremendous earthquake.

"The ground shook so violently that it knocked off the judge's wife's wig, the mayor lost his toupee, the barber dropped his scissors, the janitor his broom,

and the bear lost his tail. Now, when a bear loses his tail, he runs into the woods. The bear's woods were so thick that from one tree to the next was over a mile. So he stood by one tree and noticed that on another tree grew a tiny walnut. The bear cracked open the walnut and pulled out 346 yards of fabric. Now, when a bear possesses 346 yards of fabric, he grows rich and becomes a merchant.

"So he went to the marketplace to trade. He traded and traded, until he traded the ox, bought the goose, took home the duck, cooked the mushrooms, and ate one pea. After such a filling meal, he grew very thirsty.

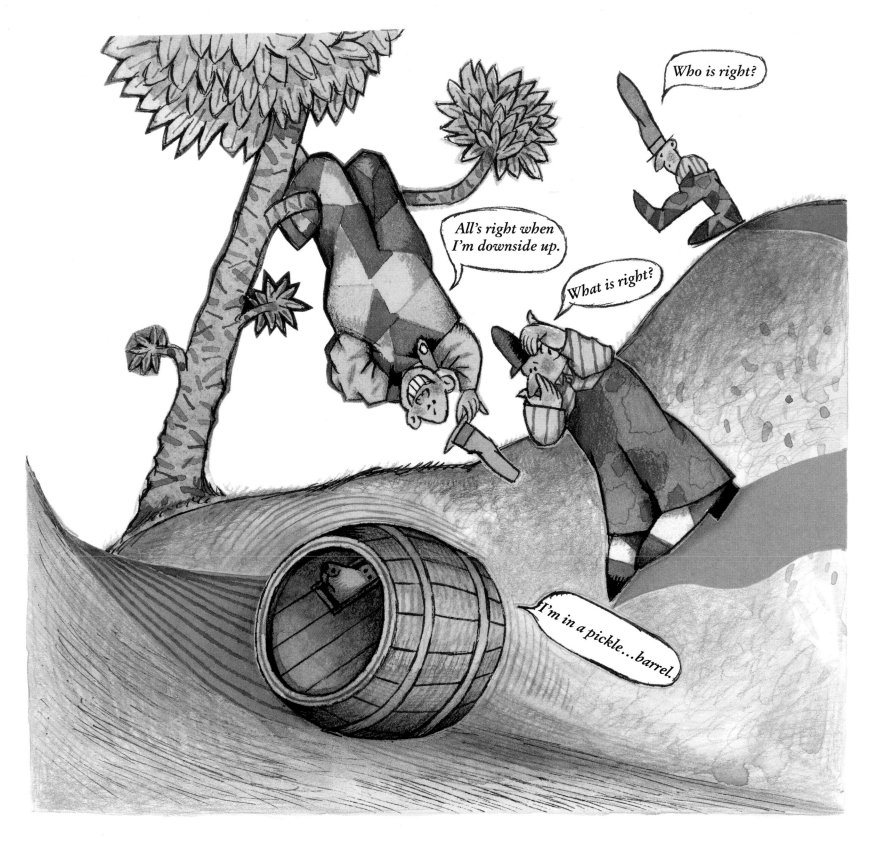

"So he bought a barrel of cider, drilled a tiny hole in it with a straw, and climbed inside. After he drank up all the cider, he grew very big and couldn't get out. So he rolled, and rolled, until he came to . . .

. . . the janitor.

"Now, on special holidays, the janitor happened to be a barrel-maker. And as this happened to be one of the most important holidays of the year, the janitor took his broom, removed two rings of the barrel, and set the bear free. When a bear is free, he grows happy. When he is happy, he grows generous. So he gave the janitor all of his remaining two inches of fabric. When the janitor was the lucky owner of the two inches of fabric, he felt rich.

"So he went to the marketplace, and there he saw the invisible half citizen with the big mustache, so he bought a tiny sardine from him. He came home, had his wife cook the sardine, and they had a great feast. He gave her the head and he ate the tail.

"A tail is an end, and this is the end of this tale, for everything has an end, except a hot dog—it has two."

By the time Lou had finished telling his tale, the traveling salesman was fast asleep and had loosened his grip. Lou got free. Before flying away, Lou called to the salesman, "Advice is for the wise; fools don't profit by it."

Lou flew to where Aunt Millie lived. When she saw him, she asked, "Why did it take you so long?"

"It's a long story," said Lou, "but since the day is long, I'll tell you how it all began."

"There once was a man, and he had twin sons. One day, he called them and said, 'Sons, nobody lives forever, and my time has come. I leave you seven goldings, a candlestick, and a broom.' And he died.

" 'He's dead,' said his sons. And while one was wiping his tears, the other quickly grabbed the goldings and the candlestick. And with a little time, a little shrewdness, and a lot of luck, he managed to become Emperor of Pickleberry.

"Now, the other son was left with the broom and became a janitor. The janitor was determined to regain their father's candlestick.

"He went to his brother and said, 'Imperial brother, please lend me soap.'

" 'Soap?' said the Emperor. 'You have a broom. What do you need soap for?'

" 'A janitor without soap is no janitor,' said the janitor.

"The Emperor reluctantly lent him a small piece of soap. The next day, the janitor came back with a large piece of soap. 'Soap grows smaller. Why is this soap larger?' the Emperor asked, surprised.

" 'Good news, brother!' said the janitor. 'Overnight, the soap grew in size.' The Emperor was pleased and took the soap.

"The janitor came to his brother and said, 'Esteemed brother, please lend me a mop.'

" 'A mop?' said the Emperor. 'You have a broom. What do you need a mop for?'

" 'A janitor without a mop is no janitor,' said the janitor. The Emperor lent him a mop. The next day, the janitor returned with two mops.

" 'Why two mops?' asked the Emperor.

" 'Good news, brother!' said the janitor. 'The mop has multiplied.' The Emperor was pleased and took both mops.

"The janitor came to his brother and said, 'Generous brother, please lend me a pail.'

" 'A pail?' said the Emperor. 'You have a broom. What do you need a pail for?'

" 'A janitor without a pail is no janitor,' said the janitor. The Emperor lent him a pail. The next day, the janitor came back with three pails.

" 'Why three pails?' asked the Emperor.

" 'Good news, brother!' said the janitor. 'The pail has tripled!' The Emperor was pleased and took the three pails.

"The janitor came to his brother and said, 'Magnanimous brother, please lend me our father's candlestick.'

" 'He who returns more than he borrows makes me richer,' thought the Emperor, and he lent him the candlestick without further questions.

"When time passed and the janitor hadn't returned the candlestick, the Emperor was furious. He marched to his brother and demanded, 'Where are my candlesticks?'

" 'Bad news, compassionate brother,' said the janitor. 'We must take the good with the bad: the candlestick has died!'

" 'Died? Impossible!' exclaimed the Emperor.

" 'Impossible?' said the janitor. 'If soap can grow, if a mop can multiply, and if a pail can triple, then surely a candlestick can die.' "

When Lou finished telling his story, Aunt Millie said, "And what did the janitor do with the candlestick?"

"Well," Lou said, "the janitor no longer sits in the dark on long winter nights. He lights a small candle and can read this story."

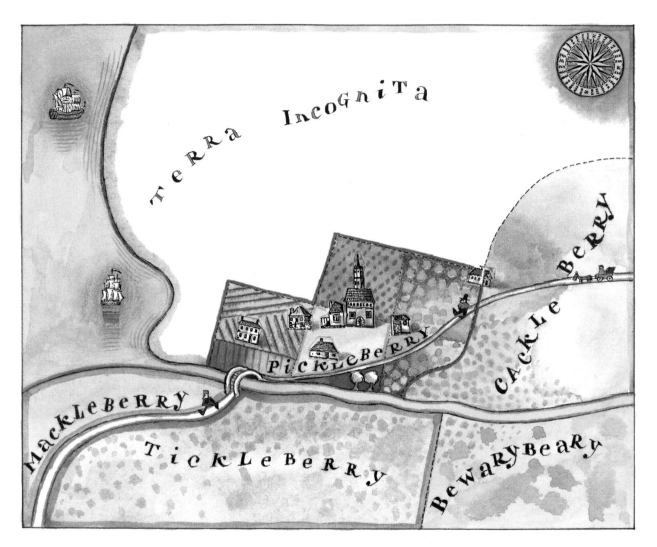

Terra Incognita

MackLeBerry

PickLeBerry

TickLeBerry

CackLeBerry

BewaryBeary

National Flag of the Empire of Pickleberry

National Sun

National Dessert—Pickle Pudding

National Moon